The Strongman

Rescue at Sea

Table of Contents

CHAPTER ONE

Wednesday afternoon, April 4

FBI Headquarters - Philadelphia

"I'm just saying, it's complete bullshit," Stewart muttered to as he walked to the President's office with his boss.

"You'd better use different words to Rickon," Salome said quietly. "That's not saying I'm disagreeing with you, but-"

"I know," snapped Stewart, then he backed off just as quickly. "Sorry. It's...it's not your fault."

They walked into the antechamber and found the president already standing there, looking grim. He beckoned them both wordlessly into his office, and Stewart handed over the sealed report.

"Sir, it's all in there as requested."

"Thank you," Rickon responded with a sigh. "An ugly business, for sure. I don't want either one of you thinking for a minute it was your fault. We all tried to talk Hank out of this, so if you're a failure, then I'm a failure, too."

Stewart glanced aside at Salome and took a deep breath. "I just...sir, it seems..."

"What? Speak freely."

"Yes, sir. In my humble opinion, it's unconscionable that we aren't telling Daven he's getting Theo and Floyd in one year. Not to mention keeping that from the boys themselves. And who's going to break the news of Hank's death to them? I just feel so wrong about this whole thing."

"Sit down and let's address all that," the president replied mildly as his hand hovered over his intercom. "Is this a tea or coffee kind of day for you?"

More like whiskey, actually. "Neither, sir, thank you. I think we should tell Daven. It will help keep him in line and out of trouble, and screw what Harmon wants. It's cruel."

The president shook his head. "It was written in the plea agreement that he wouldn't be informed, period. Hank agreed to it."

"Because he had to," Stewart replied, keeping his tone level. "His kids were being used as weapons against him. He would have signed anything!"

The president looked at Salome, then back to Stewart. "Harmon was rightly trying to protect himself. If the public knew, they would lynch him. Hell, Daven himself would probably lead the mob."

"It's cruel," Stewart repeated, not as angrily this time. "We should tell Daven anyway."

The president smiled a little, but there was nothing sinister in it. "Stewart, let me cheer you up a little. I'm going to order a full investigation of Colbert. Do you really think Harmon will help us if we break the terms of that agreement within days of signing it? He would not."

Stewart's heart leaped a little, and he was much happier suddenly. "Help us? You think he would?"

"Considering he's the one who asked me to do it, what do you think?"

Now Stewart sat up very straight. "Oh, *fuck*. Sorry, sir, I mean...he...he *asked* you?"

Rickon nodded. "You want to take it on? You can have it, but you need to keep yourself together and be objective. Can I count on you to do that?"

"Yes, absolutely. A hundred percent. On what grounds does he base his suspicion?"

"Instinct, for now. I said it wasn't enough at first, but I've had a few days to think about it. Give yourself a week to get a plan together, and in the meantime I'll call him and let him know."

"Jesus Christ," Stewart murmured as he glanced at Salome again. Her eyes were wide, clearly she was hearing this all for the first time as well.

"Sir," Salome put in, "Are we going to tell Daven that we're investigating Colbert?"

"No-"

"We have to," Stewart said quickly. "He'll quit if we don't."

"No, he won't," Salome interjected quickly.

"With all due respect, he absolutely will. I don't trust him to stay quiet, confidentiality agreement or not. He's a martyr, just like Hank. Maybe worse, because he's the opposite of impulsive, and he's going to stew about this and eventually get himself thrown in jail on purpose just to bring attention to what's happened. We'll never see it coming. And that's going to destroy his chance to have custody of the Bancroft boys."

Rickon looked alarmed. "Are you certain of that?"

Stewart nodded. "I would bet my career on it. We need to tell him now."

"I completely disagree," Salome said politely.

"You've only met him once. I know him, and Hank warned me about it several times, too. He was extremely worried that Daven would fall on his own sword."

The president held a hand up. "As the FBI, your first duty is to the investigation. But as human beings, our first responsibility is to those boys. Stewart, you can tell him. But if he breathes a word of it to anyone else, I will put him away for a long time *and* cancel the investigation. Clear?"

"Yes, sir."

The president dismissed him, and Stewart had to fight his legs to go slowly and not carry him in a flat-out run to his office.

Stewart wasn't wrong about Daven at all, even though the man hadn't mentioned the H-word in days, and he was barely on speaking terms with Rupert over it. Their last conversation had ended in a bitter fight about how fast one should move on from such a tragedy.

Rupert had to bite his tongue as he walked down the hallway to his boss's office with a new article in hand. There was nothing more he wanted than to quit, and it pissed him off that Daven had so quickly introduced a contract for him to sign in order to keep him from doing it. If he had known his friend thought so little of Hank, or that they would be unable to get along for more than 30 seconds at a time, he would have never signed.

Knock, knock. "May I come in, boss?" he asked politely.

Daven was searching for something in his closet. "Come in," came the muffled reply. "Hold on, just looking for my phone charger."

Rupert waited by the desk with newspaper in hand like he was a soldier standing guard. Daven found the item in question and went to plug it in, making no effort to speed up the process or make any kind of greeting as he sat down.

"What is it?" he finally asked.

Rupert placed the newspaper in front of him. "I know I don't have permission to talk about Hank, but what about Floyd? Look at this. Someone took a photo of him and the caption says the police were after him. We're going to get a ton of questions about this."

Daven lifted the paper, feeling his stomach turn nastily as the sight of Floyd standing alone at a crosswalk in an obviously bad part of town, looking completely lost and scared.

"What the hell?"

"There's no context or date to it, and it's so blurry that this paper didn't confirm it's him. Obviously we know it is. What do you make of it?"

Daven studied it harder, having no earthly idea what it meant. He automatically reached over to his phone and dialed Stewart.

"Daven? Wow, I was just about to call you."

"Why? Is it about this photo?"

"What photo?"

Daven swallowed hard. "Where is Floyd?" he demanded. "This says the police were after him, and he's standing alone on a corner in the snow. It's an article in the Denver Post."

"Oh. Yes, Floyd ran off when he was in Philadelphia on Saturday. We found him, he's safe now. Look, I've got to tell you something."

"*Was* in Philadelphia? Where is he now?"

"Daven, he's fine. You're not to ask about him again. Remember our agreement?"

"I want proof he's safe, or I'm talking to the press and you'll have to arrest me. Call me back when you have it."

Daven hung up the phone angrily.

"What the fuck was that?" Rupert asked hotly. "What did he say? You know you can't talk!"

Stewart called back immediately, but Daven sent it to voicemail.

"Rupert, I-"

"Now he's calling me," Rupert blurted in a slight panic as he yanked his phone out of his pocket. "I can't ignore it, Dav."

Daven took the phone and answered it himself. "What do you want?"

"If you hang up on me again, we're going to have a serious problem. Do you understand me?"

"We already have one. I want this photo explained, and I want proof Floyd is safe. This says the police were looking for him."

"They were. They found him. He's *fine*. I can't tell you anymore than that, and you know I wouldn't lie to you, nor would the president."

"You, no. But I don't trust Rickon as far as I can throw him."

Long pause. "You need to pull it together, Daven. I have news on the Colbert front."

"What?"

"We're launching an investigation of him, right now, directed by the president. The same president you just disrespected so thoroughly. He approved it over Salome's repeated objections, all because I said *you* were totally convinced of Colbert's interference and could help me prove it."

Daven was frozen in his spot, hands and face tingling from anxiety. "I see."

Stewart was furious now. "Rickon is your boss now. Not Hank, and he's *not* the enemy. I expect you to act accordingly and treat him with respect at all times. Is that also understood?"

"Yes," Daven responded coolly. "My apologies."

"Thank you. Floyd is fine." Stewart was much calmer now. "He got over-emotional and left the hotel for a short time, and got lost, but we brought him back in time to say goodbye to Hank.

There was no panic attack or anything, if that's what you're worried about."

"I was," Daven admitted quietly, greatly relieved to hear the story behind the picture.

"One last thing. You are not to breathe a single word of this investigation to a single soul. If you do, it will be canceled because then it's considered tainted. I'll update you as much as I can. Goodbye for now."

"Thank you," Daven said as he hung up the phone and handed it back to Rupert.

"What'd he say?"

Daven didn't answer; he simply reached into his desk and pulled out the original contract Rupert had signed. "I release you of this contract," he said simply as he ripped it in half, and then into quarters.

"Dav? What are you doing? Why?"

"Because I can no longer keep to my side of the agreement."

"Since when?"

Daven looked at the phone meaningfully. "You can draft your own severance package and I'll sign it without argument."

"I don't understand," Rupe prompted somberly.

”Our agreement said I have to keep you in the loop on everything. As of right now, I can no longer do that. You may leave whenever you wish.”

Rupert paused, considering it, then discarded the idea as he clapped his friend on the shoulder. “Nope. You’re stuck with me. Want to go get a beer?”

Daven covered Rupe’s hand with his own, and then gently peeled it off. “You still don’t understand. This is…I can either be your friend, or be your boss. I can’t be both at the same time.”

“Fine. Then you’re my boss from 8am-6pm, and my friend from 6pm to 8am. Now they’re not at the same time.”

“You know that’s not what I mean!”

Rupe spread his hands out in a ‘no duh’ gesture. “Yeah, I do. But don’t take the coward’s way out, Dav, and just kick me to the curb like this. You’re better than that.”

Daven considered this. “We’re just not aligned at all, it’s not going to work. I…my feelings about Hank are complicated. I’m angry at him, I’m sad, I’m everything in between…mostly angry. I just don’t want to talk about him, or the boys. It doesn’t mean I don’t care. Can you accept that?”

Rupert nodded solemnly. “Yeah. I hear you.”

"Then stop arguing with me every five seconds. I can't make a move without your disapproval, and it's driving me crazy."

"Oh, really? Have you noticed I can't even blink without you glaring at me? I'm not the one who did this to Hank, Dav. Don't take it out on me."

The two men stared at each other for a little while, then Daven backed down.

"Alright. Let's move on. Sorry, but I'll have to take a storm check for the beer."

"*Rain* check, Dav."

"And I'm going to take the rest of the week off. Unless you have any objection?"

"Of course not. I'm glad. Please get some rest."

"Call me if you need anything."

"You too, thanks."

TWO MONTHS LATER

Denver, Colorado

June 10

Harmon picked up the newspaper again and read the paragraph three times over:

In a shocking revelation brought forth by inside sources, it was discovered that the leaders of the Seditionists have collectively paid almost two million dollars out of their personal funds to cancel the deeds of 14 household servants. Additionally, all contracts the Seditionists held with the state to employ indentured labor on their campus grounds have been breached and paid off. What this means regarding the organization's stance on the Bonded Retainers Laws is unclear, but apparently we won't be seeing any more tightening of the leash under those articles. Sources say both men have now hired back several of those former servants and laborers for hourly pay and full benefits. We are working hard to confirm this and will report again tomorrow with any updates.

"Holy shit," Harmon breathed to himself quietly as he picked up the phone and dialed the leader of the Seditionists. As expected, Daven didn't pick up. In almost ten weeks he never had, nor had he answered any emails. It was almost as if the man refused to acknowledge that Harmon existed at all. Stewart hadn't interfered, either, and basically told Harmon to put on a pair of big boy pants and shut up about it.

He left another voicemail anyway.

"Daven, Harmon here. Still need to know if you want to work together on the July 1 vote. It has some measures in it related to the indentured servitude laws, as I'm sure you know. This is strictly business. Call me back when you have a moment."

Los Angeles, California

Seditionist Headquarters

Same day (June 10)

Daven was sitting at his desk alone, drinking green tea and tapping the desk incessantly with his silver pen as he read. The July 1 draft measures were out, and it was going to be a bold move to oppose them. His thoughts were interrupted by the face at the window, and he pressed the button on the desk to open the door.

"Hey. New office looks good on you," Rupert said with a small smile. Taylor slid into the office behind him.

"Thanks," Daven responded blandly. Moving into Hank's office had all but made him an emotional train wreck at first, but now he found it comforting.

"A courier was just here," Rupert said, changing the subject quickly, and he handed two envelopes to Daven. "I brought Taylor in because the first one concerns the July 1 measures. Harmon sent a handwritten note to request we cooperate with him. Says you aren't returning his calls and emails."

"Correct. But yes, we need to work with him. Taylor, let's talk later. I'll need you to lead this charge. Maybe 9am tomorrow, if that works."

Taylor nodded and left. When the door shut behind her, Daven looked at the other envelope.

"Rupert, I...I know what this is. And I don't want to open it."

"You have to."

"Open it for me?" Daven asked as he handed it back.

Rupert ripped it open. "It's a summons to report to Philadelphia to retrieve Hank's letter. You were expecting this."

"I know."

"You have to go."

"I can't. I'm going to ask Stewart to let you go get it for me. Are you okay with that?"

Rupert shook his head. "No, Dav. I think this is something you need to do yourself."

"I knew you were going to say that," Daven grumbled angrily.

"We haven't fought in two months, and I'm not going to fight you now. I'm *asking* you. Please go do this. It's what Hank wants. Maybe you'll even get a chance to talk to him and hash this out."

Daven rubbed his temples about a dozen times before responding. "Will you go with me?" he asked quietly. "Please?"

Rupe put the letter into Daven's hands, and nodded. His eyes were wet suddenly.

"Of course I'll go with you. I'll make the arrangements and coordinate with Stewart myself. Private plane?"

"Yes. Email Maurice, he'll handle it for us. I don't want anyone else to know."

"Okay. We'll get through this together, Dav."

"Thanks, Rupe. Wait…before you do anything, I think I'm going to take you up on that rain check I got back in April for a beer."

"Sounds good. I'll go pack up and pull the car around back."

CHAPTER TWO

Philadelphia

June 15

It had been four hours since Stewart quietly led Daven to his most private conference room and handed him the letter. Four hours...that's what it took for Daven to recover from his rage and let Stewart know he was ready to talk.

The man had led him into his office and sat Dav down gently, knowing this was going to be a horrifically ugly confrontation. And also knowing there was very little he could do to offer comfort.

"I'm so very sorry, Daven. There's nothing I can add to the letter. At least not while the investigation of Colbert is still ongoing. Once that's over, you'll get the uncensored version, and you'll know what I know about the boys."

"The investigation, that's right," Daven said flatly - sarcastically, rather - as he folded up the letter and put it into his inner coat pocket. "How is that going, by the way?"

Stewart cleared his throat. "I'm surprised you haven't asked me about it yet. It's been ongoing for about six weeks now. We don't have anything solid yet."

"You haven't asked for my help on anything," he responded bitterly. "I thought you said the president wanted you to work with me."

"Daven, *please* don't do this. Don't turn on me again. I'm overwhelmed as it is, and getting animosity from you won't help matters. I'm completely on my own. I can't even summon Harmon and ask for his help."

Daven didn't back down. "So...when it's discovered that Colbert was behind all this, who are you going to summon to bring Hank back from the dead?"

"That's totally unfair. He knew what he was doing, it was his choice."

"His *choice,* really? He was innocent!"

Stewart raised an eyebrow slightly. "Oh, come on. I know about those papers in his safe, which you certainly have found by now and haven't mentioned. That alone would have gotten him twenty years. So I'd tread very lightly if I were you."

"Is that a threat?" Dav bristled.

"Not at all. It's a reminder of who you worked for," Stewart answered calmly. "Hank was *far* from innocent."

"I disagree, but that's irrelevant now, isn't it? Nobody cares anyway. Tell me exactly why he gave up his kids to the state when he had the option to turn them over to me," Daven demanded.

Now it was Stewart's turn to dish out some bitter sarcasm. "Oh, I see. So this is personal. It isn't about justice. You just got your feelings hurt."

Daven shook his head in frustration. "No. You're hiding something, and I'm starting to think there's a major conspiracy going on, to be honest. This is about vengeance, not justice."

"Alright, that's it. You're done here." Stewart stood up abruptly. "I was hoping to help you understand, but it's like talking to a brick wall. You need to go before I throw you out."

Daven stood, too. "The public is going to demand answers I can't give them. I hope you're ready to be held responsible for my party's downfall."

"Me, personally? No. This is not my fault. You know what Hank's last words were to me?"

"What?"

"Stay true. You used to say that to him, he said."

Daven felt his eyes stinging. "Yes."

Stewart lowered his voice to an angry near-whisper. "I took his advice, and I trusted you. I could have been prosecuted myself for that little note I slipped you a few months ago. Never mind that - you know who I told about those papers in his safe? Nobody, because Harmon would have flipped out and stopped negotiating. Yet you still dare to stand in my office and accuse me of leading some kind of sinister conspiracy plot?"

"I didn't say you were *leading* it. Maybe you're just a pawn, too."

Stewart was red, but he kept his voice low. "Right. We're definitely done here. Go back to Los Angeles, and don't contact me again unless it's an emergency."

"You won't be hearing from me again, don't worry."

"If you're thinking of quitting, don't. You want some more bad PR? Because I can easily get an injunction that legally prohibits you from leaving. Push me any further and I'll do it right now."

Daven's nostrils flared. "I don't care. Do it, then."

"Consider it done. It'll be signed before you get on your plane. Any other insults or accusations you'd like to add before you go?"

Trust him, Dav. He's always been a friend to me.

Daven heard Hank's voice clearly in his head, as if they were standing in the same room. It startled him, and he jumped back a half-step in his dismay. The last thing he needed right now was hearing his dead friend give him unwanted advice.

"Are you alright?" Stewart asked a few moments later in true concern as he watched the blood drain from Daven's face.

"What?"

"Sit down for a minute," Stewart said as he pulled Daven's chair back out, then went to his little refrigerator under his desk. "I want you to drink some water."

Daven remained standing by the door. "I'm fine."

Stewart walked over and handed Daven the water after uncapping it. "Drink. You're white as a sheet."

"Please accept my apologies," Daven said abruptly. "I'm not being fair."

Stewart blinked in surprise. Once, then twice. "Okay. Well, that was the last thing I expected to hear. Hank told me this is how it would go and warned me to prepare for a huge fight. He definitely didn't predict an apology, though."

"I'm stressed. You don't know what it's been like for me, not knowing what happened to him."

"Really? You think Hank's only friends were you and Rupert? Maybe I wasn't as close, but I assure you this hasn't been easy for me, either."

Daven nodded. "I need to know, if...on the last day, when he was..."

"We were told it was painless and peaceful. I didn't witness it myself, thank god. But he was in good spirits that day, all things considered, if that helps you any."

"It does," Daven confirmed after a minute. "I just want to ask one more thing. It's genuine curiosity, nothing else. If you're so convinced Hank had this coming, why are you-"

"I never said he had it coming," Stewart corrected firmly. "Look, I have to stop talking now. I've already said way too much. I trust you not to make me regret it."

Daven lifted the water bottle to his lips and drank half of it in one gulp. "You won't. I'm sorry. I was being an unfair, colossal dick."

"I'm glad to see we're finally in agreement about something. But I forgive you, and I won't get that injunction if you just promise to hang in there a little longer. And to help me when I ask you, which will be soon."

"Agreed. May I let Rupert read this letter?"

"Yes. Almost forgot to mention that you and I need to talk tomorrow morning about the press statement. I'll call you at 8am your time."

"I...my apologies in advance if I'm not exactly receptive to whatever you want to say. I'll try my best not to be a dick about it, but..."

Stewart nodded sympathetically, then pushed the door open. Daven left without another word, feeling like he had just walked into someone else's life all of a sudden instead of his own.

Hank's life, actually. And it scared the hell out of him.

Daven returned to the hotel immediately, but wished he had held off. Rupert was waiting for him in the lobby, and he had no idea how he was going to break the news to him. Hadn't even thought about it, but he couldn't wait now. The sooner he got it over with, the better.

"Let's go upstairs, your room," he said darkly. Rupe nodded, but said nothing. The guards followed them, waiting a respectful distance down the hallway as the door to the room closed. Daven inhaled deeply as he took a few steps in.

"You should sit down," he said quietly, as he pulled out chairs for both of them from the dining area's table.

"Oh god," mumbled Rupert as he complied, hesitating at first to comply, but then sitting so close to Daven that their knees were touching slightly.

"I have terrible news," Daven began, his voice deeper and more enunciated that usual. "And I...honestly, I should have been spending all the time I had in the car thinking of how to break it to you, but I didn't, and that was selfish. I'm sorry, this is probably going to be...there's probably a better way I can say it...but..."

"Just tell me, Dav. It's alright."

Daven didn't look at Rupe. "Hank not only pled guilty, as we already know, he...he also chose execution instead of prison."

"Uhhh..." was all Rupert could manage for now.

"And even worse, it was carried out on March 31. He's gone, Rupe." Now Daven lifted his eyes and locked gazes with his shocked friend. "He's...it was actually his choice. I don't know why, but it's done."

Rupert swallowed a few times, but otherwise stayed calm. "Okay. Where's the letter?"

Daven wordlessly reached into his coat and handed it over, then got up to get Rupert a drink from the minibar. He thought about reaching for one of the beers, but then selected two water bottles instead and went to sit back down. Rupert took one but made no move to open it.

"They censored it," he said needlessly, pointing to the paragraph in question. "Something about the boys has been completely removed."

"Yes. I've been told I'll get the uncensored version when..." He didn't know when, so he let the sentence hang. Rupert didn't ask him to finish it.

"Right. Well, we aren't due to fly home for another three hours. Can we leave now?"

Daven nodded. "Yes, if you're feeling up for it."

"I am. Let me get my stuff together. I'll need about fifteen minutes."

Rupert didn't bring anything that would take fifteen minutes to pack, but Daven rose anyway and patted him on the shoulder, then slid quietly through the connecting door into his own suite and laid down.

His heart shattered a few minutes later when the sound of a loud sob broke into his thoughts, and he sat up and was puzzled to realize it was his own. He hadn't shed real tears yet, not even about losing the boys. The only time he'd come close to breaking was when Hank's office was unsealed a month ago and he made the mistake of going inside before it was cleared out.

But Hank's downfall hadn't been real, then. It was now.

The suite's inner door slid open from the other side as Rupert slipped in, sat down on the bed, and rested a hand on his friend's shoulder. Daven turned around and embraced him, and they held onto each other and cried for a little while.

CHAPTER THREE

Philadelphia

Rupert was absolutely dreading the plane ride home. He figured Dav would be silent, brooding, angry. Possibly even hostile. Not that he didn't have a right to be, but it was going to be a long six hours if he was any of the above.

Daven was equally dreading the trip, for different reasons. His guards Martinez and Toby were there, too, and the plane wasn't big enough to have any private conversation with Rupert. For two months - actually, almost three - Dav had remained completely silent in regards to Hank. Hadn't said a word about him, hadn't allowed anyone talk about the situation, and answered exactly zero questions publicly. Back in April the media had been in an uproar for weeks about the missing boys, but the FBI quashed that by explaining Hank had sent them to a boarding school before Daven could seek custody of them. End of story, and it blew over fairly quickly, all things considered.

Had Daven been any other man, he would have been embarrassed by that statement, possibly even self-conscious about what people would think of him. He didn't care, though. He wasn't Hank and never worried about being liked, and had no time or inclination to address it. So Rupert and Taylor forged ahead, kept in line, kept their mouths shut, and watched Daven out of the sides of their eyes while he waited impatiently for Stewart's next move.

Rupert knew something was up, of course. He never asked, but his instinct told him Colbert was being investigated. The fact that Daven couldn't tell him didn't bother him. That would have been too much of a distraction; it was better to move on, to focus on things that could be controlled, and work on getting the organization back together again.

The plane had barely leveled out at altitude before Dav turned his seat around and rested his eyes on his tired friend.

"What's the latest tally?" he asked matter-of-factly.

"53, including two more who resigned this morning," answered Rupert. That was how many people had left the organization after April's announcement that Hank wasn't coming back, and that Daven Johansson was interim CEO for a period of six months. After that, the president could approve him as a permanent replacement. The only person who knew he probably wouldn't was Daven himself, but he had never mentioned the possibility yet.

"Over ten percent now," Daven replied. "Can we run that lean?"

"Of course. We were always overstaffed anyway, you know Hank. Always paranoid about people working themselves to death, ironically enough."

Daven looked out the window and took a deep breath. It was time to tell Rupert his suspicions. "I doubt Rickon will confirm me on November 1."

"What? Why?"

"He hates me, for starters."

Rupert furrowed his eyebrows. "He does *not* hate you. Don't be overdramatic."

"Stewart said..." Daven glanced aside at the guards, who were obviously listening carefully while pretending to be totally disinterested. "Never mind. Martinez?"

The young man started, and turned with a slightly guilty expression.

"Yes, sir?"

"Have you heard from Avery? I was wondering what he's been up to."

"We went out the other night. He's with the LAPD again, working for my dad."

"Is he happy?" Daven asked mildly, and Rupert looked sideways at him in surprise. He had never heard Dav ask if *anyone* was happy, ever.

Martinez looked as if he was going to say yes just to avoid tension, but he didn't. "No, sir. He misses Hank and the boys very much. He mentioned that...."

"What?"

"He said he wanted to come see you, but he was afraid he wouldn't be welcome. He wanted to explain what happened in Philadelphia."

"Did he tell you?"

"No, sir. I'm...he wouldn't tell me a thing like that. He's very private."

Daven fell silent for a minute, then cleared his throat. "I see. Thank you for telling me. He's mistaken about not being welcome. I'll call him up when we get home."

Rupert stood up and went to flip on the television. "Let's all watch a movie. What do you feel up for, Dav?"

Daven replied glumly, "I hear they're making a film about the Titanic. It might be perfectly appropriate right now."

"Maybe so, but a tragedy is the last thing we need to watch." Rupe leaned over to examine the little cabinet full of VHS tapes and perused them carefully. "Maybe a comedy."

He finally pulled one out decisively.

"*Herbier Goes to Monte Carlo*?" Daven scoffed.

Rupert ignored him and handed the tape to the flight attendant, who cued it up for them on the player and doused the cabin lights. Daven felt rather than saw the guards watching, too, and was annoyed that they seemed delighted by the selection.

"Anthropomorphisation of cars is a silly premise for anything other than a kid's movie," Dav grumbled.

He only got a glare in return.

"Fine," Dav sighed. "Play it, then."

"This was one of Theo's favorites when he was really little. He always begged Millie put it on when she was babysitting the boys."

Daven shifted uncomfortably in his chair, feeling the eyes of the guards on him once again. He really didn't like Rupe speaking of the Bancroft sons in past tense, like they were dead, too, but there was nothing he could say about it.

"Oh. I didn't realize, sorry. I'll try to enjoy it, then."

"Thank you."

Daven didn't enjoy it, of course, and hardly paid any attention at all. He wanted so badly to take Hank's letter out of his coat and read it again. And again. And again. But he refrained, and didn't open until he got home. Then he put it in his safe and went to bed.

It would be weeks before he took it out again and noticed Hank's hastily scribbled note deep inside of the envelope, far away from the prying eyes of Stewart and Salome:

804-253-7894

It would be another two weeks before Daven saw it and called, and months before Lester would call back and agree to help him.

JUNE 30 - early morning

"Hello," said the voice on the other line. A few moments passed, then, "Hello?"

Daven cleared his throat and pitched it up a bit. "Who is this, please? Just want to make sure I have the right number."

"Nice try. Who are you?" the man demanded.

Another long pause. "I see we are at an impasse. Very well. I received your number from Hank Bancroft some time ago, but I was not in a position to call until now. Can you talk? It's important."

"I'm in a meeting. Let me take your number and call you back."

"Not possible. When is a good time to call you back?" he asked tersely.

There was a long pause.

"Okay, let me read that back to you," the man said, a note of amusement in his voice. "310-758-5100. Is that right?"

Daven's heart jolted painfully. His cell number. How the hell..? "No. I'm not sure who's number that is. When would be a good time to call you back?" he said again, trying to keep his voice steady and unconcerned.

"Actually, I'm not interested. Please remove my number from your database. Have a good day."

The angry man hung up. Daven called Taylor and Rupe to his office, brutishly admitted where he got the man's number from, and asked them to drop everything and find out who it belonged to. He dismissed Rupert's protests and sent them on their way.

Taylor came back less than an hour later, and Daven fully expected to hear it was untraceable. She dropped a sheet of paper triumphantly on his desk and crossed her arms, smiling from ear to ear.

"A certain Robert Boyd, boss. Chief Administrator of the Bonded Retainers Training School for Minors. Do you know him?"

Daven snatched the paper off the desk. Hank's old roommate and best friend. No wonder he had Daven's number. But the man was a fierce Urbane....what the hell was Hank up to now?

"Excellent work, Taylor. Where's Rupert?"

"In a PR meeting until 3pm. Do you want me to get him out?"

"No, thanks. I'll wait. Thanks. Lunch is on me today, whatever you want."

Same day - afternoon

It was the fourth time Daven had called, but the last two times he had said nothing.

"Jesus H Christ on a pogo stick. You again?" Lester scoffed. "Why don't you just talk to me? I don't bite. Not today, anyway."

Brief pause, then Daven finally spoke. "Are you the same Lester Boyd who was friends with Hank Bancroft for so long?"

"I'm going to hang up now. Goodbye."

"Just a moment, Mr. Boyd. I'm a friend of Hank's. I want the deeds to the Bancroft boys transferred to me, and I need your help to do it."

Holy shit, thought Lester, every drop of blood in his body turning to ice. He knew that voice.

"Absolutely not," he blurted harshly. "You really think I'm going to give them over to you assholes to brainwash for the next twenty years?"

"So they *are* there, then. Excellent."

Fuck ! Lester breathed under his breath, furious at himself for falling into such a simple trap. It took him a minute to collect himself; visions of losing his job and being blackmailed by the Seditionists were already filling up his darkest thoughts.

"Screw you, you stupid son of a bitch," Lester muttered angrily.

Daven was clearly unmoved by the insult. "Don't worry, I won't tell anyone you fell for that."

Lester slammed down the phone, which rang again less than a minute later. He picked up with shaking hands.

"You should seriously consider cooperating with me," Daven said politely. "Hank Bancroft was framed. We have proof now, and I'm going to submit it to the FBI soon. It's too late to save Harmon and Colbert, but not the boys."

"You've picked the wrong man to bully, idiot," Lester interrupted hotly, hating that he was so rattled he couldn't think of anything better to say. *Framed?* Not possible; the Seditionists were just getting desperate now and trying to mess with his head.

Daven retorted with a hint of regret in his tone, "As I said, I'm a friend in this particular discussion. To both you *and* the Bancrofts. Hank made it clear that you were a man who cares deeply about their welfare, if nothing else."

"What discussion? You can't have them, and you're nuts if you think I'm going to waste one more second on you. Lose my number, pal."

Daven replied casually, "No. I'm not giving up until they're safe with me, no matter what it takes."

"Don't you fucking threaten me," Lester warned. "I had nothing to do with any of this."

"I understand that. But I need your help. Please."

Complete silence from Lester's side invaded the line for at least a minute, then he finally said, "No. Hank was guilty as hell, and you know it. You're the one who turned him in!"

" *What?*" Daven was astonished. "I absolutely did not. Who told you that? Harmon? Colbert?"

"Oh come on, Johansson. Stop the bullshit. Don't ever call me again. Especially don't ever threaten me again."

There was a brief silence on the other end of the line, and then a slight huff. "You've completely misunderstood my intentions. I'm not threatening you."

"Could've fooled me!" Lester practically yelled.

"Mr. Boyd...I did not turn Hank in. He was framed. I don't know how much clearer I can be."

"Look, Johansson, you're in deep shit. I know you are breaching the plea bargain just by calling me, so you're headed for jail time, my man, as soon as I let Harmon know. Start packing."

"I'm perfectly aware of what they could do to me, and I'm willing to risk it because Hank said you could be trusted. If you tell Harmon, I won't deny anything. I'll go to jail for this. Hank gave me your number in his very last communication with me, and he *never* would have put either of us in danger for no reason. I don't know why. You do. Call me back when you're willing to talk about the future of Theo and Floyd."

The call terminated before Lester could get another word in.

Daven sucked in his breath and held it for a long time, toying with the notion that he'd just made a huge, life-changing mistake. Lester knew there was a plea bargain, and he apparently knew what the terms were. He *knew*, while he claimed to have nothing to do with it. Hank had either dug Daven's grave or Lester's with his little note. And Daven realized it was probably going to be his, if he couldn't get Lester to work with him, and fast.

Fuck...

CHAPTER FOUR

Richmond, Virginia

BRTSM

Lester Boyd had, of course, fallen in love with the boys again as soon as they'd arrived back in April. He was relieved neither one of them seemed to have inherited the worst of their father's characteristics. They hadn't exactly inherited the best ones, either. Theo was lazy, Floyd was meek, and both the boys together were not much of a force to be reckoned with at first.

At first.

Something had changed in Floyd a while back, almost immediately after Lester had first heard from the mysterious caller who later turned out to be Daven. Floyd had been standing in Lester's office when that call came through, so at first Lester thought maybe he had heard the voice through the phone and figured out who was calling. It quickly dawned on him that of course Floyd would have recognized the phone number that Lester was stupid enough to blurt out loud for all to hear.

If that was the case, though...why didn't the boy saying anything, and why did he lose his openness and sweetness so quickly? Lester had seen the change the very next day, and it was bothering him so much that he had to nearly physically hold himself back from asking what the hell was up. The way Floyd held himself straight as a ramrod, the way he physically but subtly blocked Theo protectively...even the new tension in response to all but the mildest questions. It was almost as if he was scared to death that Daven had called. No, not scared. Angry. It made no sense whatsoever; Hank had mentioned time and again how close the boys were to Johansson and how much being separated for a year would hurt them.

Lester had wanted to tell the boys, of course, that Daven would take them out if this awful situation in a year. But he couldn't, and he certainly wouldn't anyway now that he suspected Floyd hated the man.

So Lester was distracted. It had been five weeks since Daven called to tell him Hank was allegedly framed. Thirty-five long, stressful days since Lester learned exactly why the new leader of the Seditionists was infamous for being approximately as subtle as a machine gun. In that time, Lester had quietly read up about him and pored over dozens of videos and news clips. The amount of material on him was limited, but it was enough that he felt almost knew Johansson personally now, and it disturbed him that something wasn't adding up.

Johansson definitely didn't seem to have the imagination or balls required to make up wild, unprovable theories out of the blue for no reason. He was also strictly forbidden from trying to find out where the boys were. And yet, he had done just that, at the risk of certain jail time and public shame and infamy. Nobody would do that unless they were one hundred percent convinced they were absolutely right. Not to mention it was extremely odd that he apparently didn't know the boys were going to be his in one year.

But then again, Hank possessed a masterful ability to manipulate anyone into believing anything; it was part of the reason he was so successful in politics even when he was pushing back against popular opinion. This could all be a trick. Perhaps he'd even brainwashed Daven into believing there was some kind of conspiracy. But why? He was guilty, after all. He'd never said he wasn't...

The only thing holding back Lester from telling Colbert that Daven had called was the fact that he'd inadvertently given up the boys' location to him. That alone would cost him his job. Every day since then, Lester had discreetly kept a set of boxes nearby to be ready for filling when the time came that he was inevitably asked to leave.

Nothing had come of it, though. Strangely, there was no further contact from Daven, which only strengthened Lester's curiosity and doubts rather than quashing them.

But he did nothing about it. Yet.

"Theo."

"Mmmmummph."

"*Theo*. Move over."

Theo opened one eye and peered at his brother, barely visible in the gloom. "Nightmares again?" he asked sleepily as he backed up against the wall to make room.

"Not a nightmare," Floyd clarified as he slid in bed next to his brother and held on tightly to him to keep from falling out. "An idea."

"Shhhhh. Oh god. What? Your last idea got both of our butts blistered."

Floyd sighed. "I'm sorry, okay? I've said it like a million times. Can you stop bringing that up?"

"No."

"I'm going to tell Mr. Boyd we know who he is."

"What? Why?"

"Because maybe he'll give us some news on dad. If we befriend him, start reminiscing, you know...maybe we can win his confidence eventually. Or he'll feel sorry for us, or something. And help us."

"Help us *what?* Floyd, it's 3am. And you always told me he hated dad."

Just as he said that, the overhead light came on and blinded them both painfully.

"Ow," Floyd moaned as he hurriedly got on his feet and shaded his eyes to look at the culprit.

"Mr. Bancroft," said the night manager of the dorm, quietly. "Back to bed."

"Mr. Donatello-"

"Nope. Out you go."

Floyd's sighed and looked around the room as Theo's three roommates woke and grumbled at him, rubbing their eyes painfully. He patted Theo on the head and walked back to his room, which he shared with no one at the moment, and flopped onto his back in the creaky bed.

"Sir, can't I just...there are two empty beds in here. Why can't I share with Theo? He's my brother."

"You'll have to take that up with Mr. Boyd." The man paused, then seemed to have a sudden deep thought and walked in the room to sit down on the bed opposite Floyd. "I haven't heard anything about your father yet."

Floyd stared at the ceiling. "I know. I...I really appreciate you trying to find out for me. I know I say that all the time, but it really means a lot. Thank you."

"Happy to help, but you know what I would appreciate in return? For you to stop fucking around and putting you and your brother in danger. Next time this happens, I have report you. No choice. Understood?"

Floyd turned on his side to study the older man he had become so friendly with over the past few weeks. "Deal. I'm sorry. But he's my brother-"

"Yes, I know, but it's not fair to the other boys to keep giving you special treatment. I've said it before, and I really mean it this time."

"Do you know Daven Johansson?" Floyd blurted suddenly, without thinking.

"Not personally, of course. What's he like?"

"He's a dick," Floyd replied blandly. "And he's the reason me and Theody are here in the first place. Mr. Boyd said I could write a letter to him so I did, but I haven't asked him to send it yet."

Donatello crossed his arms. "Are you upset with him for not seeking custody of you and Theo?"

"No! I'm glad he didn't, oh my god. That would be horrible."

"So what did you put in the letter, then?"

Floyd sat up again and pulled the sheaf of paper out from between his mattresses. "I asked him why he...why he turned dad in. They were best friends. He was my uncle. In name, I mean, not blood. Then he called here to talk to Mr. Boyd, and-"

"He called *here*?" interrupted Donatello, shocked. "He knows you're here? Floyd, who else have you told about this?"

"Nobody," answered Floyd quickly, a little hurt at his new friend's harsh tone. "I mean, Theo knows, but-"

Donatello stood up abruptly. "Okay, Floyd. Keep it to yourself from now on. I'm sorry, but I can't continue this conversation, ever. Don't bring him up again, and don't tell anyone else he called. Goodnight."

"Sir, wait…" Floyd called as the man started to leave. Then he swallowed hard as the light was shut off and the door closed abruptly, leaving him alone once again. He laid back on the bed, his eyes stinging with tears, and lay awake until dawn, staring at the ceiling and feeling his heart harden just a little more towards the man he had once called Uncle Dav.

Of all the conversations Lester Boyd had dreaded in all his life, this one had to rank at the top of the list. He tensed as Floyd - who was in trouble yet *again* for mouthing off to his teachers - trudged in sleepily and flopped into a chair before being given permission.

"What's this all about?" Floyd blurted moodily. "It's fucking 7 o'clock in the morning."

Lester gulped and leaned over to pick up his short cane. "Stand up," he ordered briskly.

"No."

"I would comply if I were you, kiddo."

Floyd eyed him dangerously. "I'm not afraid of you anymore, *Uncle Lester.*"

Lester paused, set the cane down and crossed in front of the desk, then leaned back against it. His heart was beating so hard that it was making him dizzy, and Floyd's ferocious glare wasn't helping matters.

"How long have you known?" Lester asked quietly, after taking a few moments to gather his wits.

Floyd said nothing. He just stared.

"I gather Theo doesn't remember."

Again, dead silence from the elder Bancroft boy.

Lester threw up his hands. "Alright. So you know. What now, you're going to be a little shit from now on just to get back at me for-"

"Why did Daven turn in my dad and send us here? Did he have some kind of agreement with you? Were you two secretly conspiring against him this entire time?"

"Lower your voice. I don't know what you're talking about."

Floyd laughed humorlessly. "I knew it. There's no other reason he would have called here, but you're not allowed to talk to him, are you? That's why Mr. Donatello freaked out when I mentioned it to him."

"You did *what?* Floyd, what the holy hell has gotten into you?" Lester blurted, his hands raised up in the pre-surrender stage. "I've been nothing but nice to you since the day you-"

"I want Theo assigned to my room. Just the two of us, for the rest of our time here. That's the price for my silence. Take it or leave it."

Lester stared at him for several long, tense moments. "You've got me wrong, kiddo. I don't know what you think is going on, but-"

"Don't lie! And don't call me that. My name is Floyd." Floyd started to choke up a little, and Lester subconsciously wrung his hands together in his anxiety.

"Okay," Lester said patiently, "you can room with Theo, but we're going to have a long talk first."

Floyd stood up quickly, his expression still dark and dangerous. "No. We're done here. Have a nice day."

Lester stared in amazement as Floyd confidently strode out and disappeared. That was the exact moment Lester realized he was wrong about Floyd not having inherited Hank's temperament and worst traits. Wrong about being grateful the kid had gone a different direction.

Well. Turned out Floyd was going to be *just* like Hank, if this was any indication. *Shit..*

Floyd never spoke to Lester again on his own accord. He politely answered yes or no questions, left it at that, and broke no more rules. He was polite and obedient to the point of near absurdity, although the deepset restlessness in his manner never wavered.

There was only one time Lester started to go after him; Floyd was being uncommonly hard on Theo for the tenth time in a week it seemed, but the teenager was clearly in "big brother protective mode." It was working since Theo had started to finally fall in line, too, so Lester let it go with a few mild words of warning which Floyd clearly intended to ignore.

Then Daven called back, unexpectedly, on an otherwise sunny day when Lester was finally feeling at peace with himself and his role in Hank's death.

"Mr. Boyd."

"Yes?" Lester replied patiently, although his heart began galloping like a racehorse going downhill.

"The FBI has prematurely ended their involvement in the investigation of Colbert."

"I don't know what you're talking about," Lester lied. "Stop calling me-"

"The agent responsible for the work has been fired," Johansson replied flatly.

"How is that any of my business?"

"Because I learned something very interesting last week. You were Harmon's negotiator for the plea bargain. Yet, last time we talked, you claimed to know nothing and that you had nothing to do with any of this."

Oh, fuck.

"So," continued Daven, "the fact that you lied tells me my initial instincts were correct. You were conspiring with Colbert and Harmon to frame Hank. Perhaps to get back at him for the way your friendship ended eleven years ago. Or because Colbert tricked you into his scheme, which I find far more likely."

Lester quickly hung up the phone and unplugged it for safe measure. Then he went to the empty office next door and shakily dialed Colbert.

CHAPTER FIVE

Los Angeles, California

Seditionists HQ

On a normal day, it took quite a lot to get Daven irritated. On a stressful day, it took very little. But he had never before yelled at any employee, no matter what the impetus. In fact, sometimes he would get calmer and quieter in inverse proportion to how much a situation was blowing up out of control. Disarming people with his refusal to fight was one of his greatest talents.

Today was a new day. He had started off the morning with a full-fledged shouting match with Rupert, followed by a phone-shouting match with Salome Danby, followed by the reprise of another shouting match with Rupert just before 5pm. Half the office had heard them all and most of them looked about ready to vacate the premises, as if a bomb threat had been called in.

"Dav, for the last time, you *cannot* make that call," Rupert fumed as he slammed his hand down on the desk for the second time today. "Are you out of your fu...out of your mind?"

Daven set his pen down and glared across the table. "You were warned, Rupe. I told you that you wouldn't like what was going on, and you agreed to stay out of it as long as I kept you informed. I've kept you informed, so keep your end of the bargain and *stay out of it!*"

"Absolutely not. Fuck it all, Dav, you're just asking to get yourself thrown in jail. I can't run this goddamned loony bin by myself, so-"

"That's enough."

Rupert didn't relent. "So you just...you're just going to tell Salome you've been in contact with Lester Boyd. For months."

"Not months. Three calls, over three months."

"Same thing. Jesus Christ, you're just like Hank. You know that? Not a shred of common sense, and everything done out of some horribly skewed sense of duty and honor." Rupert had broken into a sweat, and he was angrier than Daven had ever seen him. "You always said Rickon wouldn't confirm you in November anyway. So I suppose you think you have nothing to lose now, is that it? Fuck it all?"

"Pretty much, yes," Daven admitted, which completely threw Rupert off guard.

"What...wait, no," he stuttered. "You're trying to confuse me."

"No, I'm trying to shut you up so I can make this call before Salome leaves the office."

Rupert reached out and snatched up Daven's cell phone. "I'm not giving this back to you until you agree to think about it over the weekend. If you're still intent on committing harakiri, at least do it Monday morning so you don't ruin her weekend. Or mine."

Daven bristled. "I am *not* like Hank, by the way. If you ever say that again, our friendship is over. I would have *never* given up my kids the way he did. Nor treated them the way he did. *Never*. He chose to give them to Harmon over me, and you dare to say I'm just like him?"

Rupert crossed his arms and took a step back. "I get it now. This is personal. You don't give a shit about our party anymore, do you? You're just pissed at Hank because you got your feelings hurt, and-"

"I have to do what's right, Rupert, and to be bluntly honest, your opinion of *why* I'm doing it doesn't matter. Especially when you don't know all the facts."

Rupe nodded, his anger leveling out somewhat. "Fair enough. So you're going to tell Salome how you've been investigating on your own against FBI mandates, and let her know that you've been interfering and working secretly with Stewart on the side. Is that all, or is there more? Oh, by the way...if you do that, I will quit on the spot."

Daven slowly walked over to Rupert and lowered his voice to a near-whisper.

"Fine, I'll tell you what's upsetting me. Stewart was fired this morning because he accidentally let it slip to me that Lester Boyd was Harmon's negotiator. The investigation is now over."

Rupert's jaw dropped. "Holy shit. Dav...I..."

Daven continued, "Obviously, that opens up an entirely new set of questions that will have to be answered. The reason I'm calling Salome now is take all the blame and offer to resign if she re-hires Stewart to continue the investigation, and start a new one on Lester Boyd. So, if you quit..."

Rupert nodded, then took a few minutes to stare out the window and gather his thoughts. He didn't move a muscle, and neither did Daven as he sat behind his desk, watching thoughtfully and feeling like he had just swallowed an anvil.

Rupert said eventually, very quietly, "I'm sorry, Dav. You have to do what you can live with. I won't quit."

"Thank you. If it's any consolation, she's not going to take the offer. But I have to ask."

"Hmmm. Wait...three calls to Lester Boyd now? Did you call him again, even though you swore to me you wouldn't?"

"Yesterday. It didn't go well. He hung up on me."

"You...you lied to me."

"I broke a promise, actually. Not the same thing, but you have a right to be angry about it if you need to."

Rupert turned around, walked slowly up to the desk, and didn't take his eyes off his friend. "I see. When you explain this to Salome, kindly confirm to her that I had nothing to do with any of this whatsoever, and that you're acting against my express wishes and advice."

"I will, of course. I may be a lost cause, but your standing in this organization is intact, and I intend to keep it that way."

Rupert was stone-faced. "Well, you're right about one thing. My standing is all we've got left now."

Daven eyed him worriedly, and started to reply, but he could thinking of nothing. Rupert turned and left the office, shutting the door quietly behind him.

Daven didn't call Salome. He snuck out after the conversation with Rupert and went home to think about it.

Hank's home, rather. He had sold his own in August, and Hank's old house was on the market now with several offers. The boat was gone, too, and all the cars except for the Thunderbird. Every dollar had gone towards the staggering bills he and Rupert had received from canceling the deeds to their household servants. The money for the second house would go straight into a irrevocable trust for the boys, Daven had already decided, so that their owner would have the money to cancel their deeds when they reached the halfway point. Floyd would be 26, and Theo would be 22.

For the hundredth time as he greeted his dog and his two fosters (it didn't feel right saying Starsky and Hutch were actually *his* now), he wondered how the boys were doing now, and what their future could possibly be like. They'd never see their dogs again if he didn't succeed in his mission to vindicate Hank. It almost didn't bear thinking about.

Maurice met him in the living room and took his coat and briefcase away.

"Thanks, Maurice. Sorry I didn't let you know I was coming home early. Any news on the real estate front?"

"No sale yet. The offers keep piling up, it's quite amazing. Everyone wants a piece of Hank's history, apparently."

"Well, he did live there for ten years. That's understandable."

Maurice was no longer servant and was a well-paid employee who considered Daven a friend, but old habits never died hard. He started to ask a question, gulped a little, then ignored his pounding heart as he forged on.

"Any news of Hank and the boys?" he asked, just the same way he did every single day, and had done so for months.

"I'm afraid not," Daven replied automatically as he sat down to untie his shoes. "If the bills are ready to sign, go ahead and head home early. I'll take care of the dogs."

Maurice hesitated. "I'm sorry to keep asking. Are we ever going to know what happened to him?"

Daven stopped what he was doing, and considered the guarded question. Maurice had loved Hank and the boys, and it was increasingly unfair to keep the poor man in the dark.

"I know that you're really asking me *when* I'm going to tell you what happened to him."

Maurice nodded slightly, his expression worried.

"I can't, by law," Daven admitted shortly. "Sorry for not saying it plainly before. When I can, you will be among the first to know."

"I understand, sir. Are the boys ever coming back?"

"Don't call me sir. No, they're not. I've explained this to you already. I didn't seek custody of them."

Maurice flushed. "Right, sorry. On another subject, I'm sure you already know but I just wanted to remind you that Avery is coming over for lunch tomorrow."

Daven had actually forgotten completely, and again he was reminded of the many times he'd scoffed when Hank had insisted he'd need to keep a secretary at home once he was leading the party. Of course, the man had been absolutely right, Daven conceded begrudgingly. His life would have fallen to pieces a dozen times over already without Maurice to manage his schedule.

"Thank you, I'd forgotten. What time?"

"12:30. Chef said he sent you an email asking about the menu but you never replied, so I told him to make chicken piccata."

Daven swallowed hard as he set his keys into the drawer of the side table. That had been Floyd's favorite meal.

"I'm sorry, he'll have to make something else. I'll go talk to him. See you tomorrow."

"I'm sorry. I thought that was one of your favorites. My apologies if-"

"No, no," Daven interrupted politely. "It is. But I've had it for lunch two days in a row."

Maurice smiled, relieved that he hadn't made another mistake. Daven could be impossible to read sometimes. "Oh, I understand. Tomorrow's Saturday, by the way. I'll see you Monday."

"Right, thanks. Goodnight."

Daven found Chef and requested he go out to buy a few nice steaks, then went into the guest bedroom (he couldn't bear to move to the master suite yet) and fell sound asleep for almost two hours. He dreamed about Hank and the boys, as usual.

Richmond, Virginia

Colbert hadn't picked up the phone. Lester wasn't sure whether to be relieved or upset; he wasn't sure he'd find the courage to dial those numbers again. He certainly knew he wouldn't have the courage (or stupidity) to ever dial Daven back. Besides, what on earth would he tell him?

Friday nights at BRTSM were no fun for the school's 200 boys. It was always the most rigid formal dinner training, when they practiced serving and waiting. Like stuffy British footmen of old, outdated and relics, Lester always said to himself. But that was what the clients demanded, and so the school provided. The food was too rich, the service too formal, the conversation too stifled. He much preferred the staff dining room.

He dressed up every week, however, and put his best face forward as he walked into one of the fake-gilded dining rooms that served well for training. He had a one-in-five chance of being seated at the table where the Bancrofts were assigned, and to his dismay, found that he'd indeed beaten the odds. Floyd was stationed directly behind his chair, looking sharp but remarkably sullen in his dress uniform. Lester half expected to be garroted before dessert, he realized wryly. Theo was across the table, but he had a different expression altogether; it was more of a sad resignation and acceptance.

Lester looked up and down the table of 20, ten people to each side. All of them except himself were teachers eager to show off their new charges to the assistant dean; the same one who wanted to be anywhere else but here. He sat back as Floyd unfolded the napkin and laid it deftly over his lap.

"Thank you," he said automatically as he reached for his water. This was the second-most advanced table for training, the boys having already graduated from serving 7-course meals and were now trying out a 9-course meal for the first time. Their next move would be to the 12-course meal table, but that wouldn't be for at least four or five weeks. They had to master this first.

Lester didn't taste the first five courses. He was hyper-aware of Floyd's presence, made worse by the fact that he couldn't see his face 99% of the time. The elder Bancroft was perfection, however, and spilled nothing and made no mistakes. Theo, on the other hand, was a nervous wreck and couldn't seem to get anything right. He was soon removed from the table by the butler, and was seen no more. Lester wasn't worried; the boy would get some refresher lessons to give him a boost of confidence and be back next week.

Lester finally caught Floyd's eye as he set down the main course.

"You're doing well, son," he murmured quietly, approvingly.

Floyd froze. "I'm not your son," he replied sharply, a little too loudly. Lester's dining table neighbors looked up in horror as Floyd stepped back and reached for the next plate.

"I haven't had lamb in ages," Lester announced with a fake-plastered grin to those who were watching him. "Looking forward to this one."

He didn't taste the lamb, either. When the next course was placed in front of him, he carefully avoided making eye contact with his angry server. It took him a few seconds to realize it wasn't Floyd at all, and he looked up in surprise at the Butler, who saw his confusion and rushed over to his side.

"Something wrong, sir?" the coat-tailed man asked very discreetly as he bent over to speak directly into Lester's ear.

"Where did Floyd go?" Lester whispered neutrally. "He was doing a really good job."

The butler looked amazed. "Sir? I...he was taken away for discipline, of course."

"That's not necessary, Paul. Bring him back, please."

"But, I...it's already...we've already sent him off, sir. My apologies."

Lester nodded and let it go. He had never known a dessert and mignardise to last so long in his life. It felt as though three hours had passed before the interminable meal ended and he could get back to his office. Floyd was outside the door, of course, waiting obediently in the "chair of doom" that he had been getting to know all too well lately.

Lester walked up carefully and then sat down on the bench next to him, not even remotely upset that the teenager wouldn't meet his eye. It was understandable.

"I shouldn't have called you son. Next time I'll be more careful."

Floyd looked aside at him with red-rimmed eyes. "You could have told the head butler that before he...before he.."

Lester glanced down at Floyd's welted palms and felt a surge of anger, but it would be inappropriate to sympathize right now. He hardened his voice instead. "He did his job when you messed up yours. You knew better. Got to control those impulses. Alright, you're forgiven. Just so you know, Theo isn't in trouble. Just had a bit of a bad night, it happens."

"Oh, right. So he can have one, but I can't?"

"You know it's not the same thing. I have some Advil in my office, if you want it. Will take the edge off the sting."

"No."

Lester shrugged. "Alright, well...you did a really good job tonight, otherwise. I was impressed."

Floyd said nothing; he was thinking about the servants who used to serve him and Theo.

Lester decided to take the plunge while Floyd was here and pretty much his captive audience. He might not have a chance otherwise.

"Floyd," he said quietly. Gently. "Your dad sent you here because he knew I'd look after you and take good care of you. I'm really trying my best, kiddo. I had nothing to do with the crimes he was charged with. None whatsoever. I need you to hang in there and get past this."

"Then why was Daven calling you and why is it all a secret," Floyd asked flatly, not even phrasing it as a question. He was already convinced of his conspiracy theory and didn't need an explanation.

"Your dad left him my number so he could call and check up on you guys. I didn't know that when he first called, I mean...when you boys were standing in my office. He and I were never friends, let's just put it that way. He's the last person I wanted to talk to at the time."

Floyd turned to look at Lester now. "To check up on us? Why? He doesn't give a shit about us. I hate him. Tell him we're dead."

Lester shook his head in confusion. "I don't know why you would say that. Your dad told me you treated Daven like an uncle, and vice versa. What on earth happened to make you hate him?"

"He turned dad in and made us slaves, maybe? No big deal," Floyd jeered, and Lester sat up a little bit taller.

"Floyd...who told you that?"

"Hailey Hendricks."

"The shit reporter? *Hailey?* You listened to *her*?" Lester was shocked. He didn't follow politics anymore, but even he knew Hailey was trash.

"It was...it was on the news," Floyd said, faltering a little.

"Look," Lester said with a sigh, "you're sixteen years old. Almost seventeen. I'm not going to talk to you like you're a child anymore, okay? Do you want to speak as adults?"

"Yes," Floyd replied after a moment, looking as scared as a toddler all of a sudden.

"Reporters lie sometimes. They work for network brass who get paid to pay other people to say what they think people want to hear. Hailey is the worst of the worst, downright corrupt, and she was lying. I can tell you that with a hundred percent certainty."

Floyd seemed amazed and confused. "What?"

"I'm also going to tell you - adult to adult - that I'm putting my job on the line by telling you all this. I work for the Urbanes. Do you think they'd want me telling you their reporters are liars?"

"No. I mean, I knew anyway, kind of. That's why my dad would never let me watch the news."

"Smart man."

Floyd sat up straight. "Alright, then I just have one more question."

"Sure."

"Daven was me and Theo's guardian. So why did our dad choose to have us enslaved rather than sent to his house to live, if he was such a good guy?"

The hair on Lester's neck raised up a little at that question, and his stomach churned uncomfortably. He was suddenly ill-at-ease again over his part in the negotiation.

"I don't know, Floyd. I really don't. If I had been a fly on the wall at the FBI, I could tell you."

"Well, I don't believe you. If you'd seen how he was acting, and the way he refused to defend dad...."

Lester shrugged again, but his throat was tight. "Well, I'm telling the truth. Not much else I can say about it."

"I eavesdropped on one of his calls with Daven once, just before he left," Floyd said quietly. "It was an accident. He didn't know I was under his desk. I'd been playing hide and seek with Theo and dad came in talking on his cell phone. We weren't allowed in his study."

"Did he find you?"

"No. He was really angry already, and I didn't want to make him madder, so I just stayed there. He told Uncle Dav that Colbert was going to keep his promise to him, as he always knew he would even after ten years."

"Promise to what?"

"To visit him in jail. I never knew they were friends after everything that happened during the Revolution. Thought they were enemies, but Dad never really told me anything about work. I just...sometimes I feel like I don't know him at all."

The hair on Lester's neck raised even higher. "Wait. He said that ten years ago Colbert made a promise to visit your dad in jail?"

"Yes."

"That's...are you sure that's what he said?"

Floyd nodded, then wiped his nose with the back of one hand. "I'm sorry, I really miss...I just...I want to go home."

Now Lester's eyes were moist, too. "I know. I'm sorry."

"I never thought I would miss him this much. He can be so mean to me and Theo sometimes." He looked down at his welted hands in disgust. "But at least he never does *this*."

"Yeah...that's something, at least," Lester agreed helplessly. "You can go back to your room now."

After Floyd left, Lester went into his office and sat down hard, trying not to think of the poor kid bursting into tears. He was already distracted anyway by something Colbert had said long ago - during their first meeting about the trial - suddenly tugged at the edges of his consciousness, but never quite fully formed itself. Like trying to remember the voice of someone long dead, he mused grimly. He tried hard to remember, then gave up, laid his head on his arms, and began dozing on the edges of a dream.

A few minutes later he awakened abruptly, the stark memory of the only words Colbert had ever said about his Seditionists informant suddenly ringing clear in his head like a church bell:

The man talks like a goat with a banana stuck in his throat, but he has all the right access to get shit done.

The right access to get shit done. That didn't mean what he thought it meant...did it?

If there was even a possibility it did, though...

It was a few minutes before midnight when Lester drove into town with a long coat over his suit, praying the entire time that he wasn't losing his fucking mind by jumping to the crazy conclusions he was currently coming to. He spotted a gas station far from his usual haunts and pulled over. Nobody would recognize him here, and there were no cameras.

It was 12:35am. He took a deep breath, cursed under his breath for a little while, then picked up the pay phone and dialed Daven. He was so nervous it took him three tries to get the number in correctly.

Los Angeles

Rupert Aster house, 9:50pm

Daven strode up the front stairs two by two just as the front door opened. As usual, he didn't think to call first, but the Johansson guards had given the Aster guards a heads-up that the boss was on the way over, and Rupert had hastily gotten dressed and ran down to intercept him just in time.

"Everything okay, Dav?" Rupe asked fearfully as his friend reached him and grabbed his arm in a tight grip. He noticed his guards jump and move slightly towards him, but he quickly warned them off with a slight shake of his head.

Daven was almost breathless. "Who do we know that talks like *a goat with a banana stuck in his throat?*"

Rupert stared at him in shock. "What the....?"

"It's a serious question, Rupe. Think on it," Daven urged. "Quickly."

Rupe shook his head like a dog. "Alright. Uh. There's...that strange fellow in accounting, you mean?"

"Exactly. Yannick. He's been working with Harmon and Colbert this whole time. Probably still is."

"Holy shit," Rupe whispered back fiercely. "That fucker!"

"Come with me to the office. I'll have Taylor and Shane meet us there."

"Yeah, of course. Give me a couple minutes, got to finish dressing and tell Millie."

"I'll tell her. Where is she?"

"Uh, in the tub."

Daven blushed instantly. "Never mind, I'll wait in the car. Hurry."

CHAPTER SIX

Los Angeles

"I think I scared your guards," Daven observed nonchalantly on the way to the office.

"You did. They'll get over it." Rupe was a nervous wreck. Vance was driving them in the truck, which didn't have privacy glass, so Daven hadn't explained anything yet.

"This traffic," Rupert complained a few minutes later - again - unable to keep his silence for more than a minute at a time. He knew he was getting on Daven's nerves, but he couldn't help it. "10 o'clock at night. Don't these people have to work tomorrow? We've gone less than a mile."

Vance replied quickly, "Going as fast as I can, sir. Santa Monica Boulevard down to 10th Street is closed for a film shoot."

"Oh. Thanks. That wasn't a criticism, by the way," he added belatedly. Vance said nothing.

Daven glanced meaningfully at Rupe; it was one of his many trademark looks that needed no words. This one in particular was the ' *calm down before you give yourself a stroke'* version.

"It's Friday night, in Los Angeles. Of course there's traffic."

"Why didn't we take the Escalade?" Rupert complained. "You're killing me here."

"Rupert," Dav mumbled warningly as he looked up again from scrolling through emails on his phone.

"You know, our party's own policies forbid you from using personal vehicles while conducting company business. It's not safe."

Daven bristled a little. "Not safe for me, or for you?"

Rupert rolled his eyes. "Fine. Sorry. I'll shut up."

"Thank you. I took this car to try to keep the press from tailing us. No use getting them worked up into a frenzy about why we're going to the office on a Friday night."

"Oh. You could have just said that."

"I would think it was obvious," Daven shot back.

Vance cleared his throat and glanced backwards at them through the mirror. "Sorry to eavesdrop. We're being followed by at least 3 cars I recognize."

Daven resisted the urge to look backwards. "No need to apologize. Thank you. Please go to Taylor's instead of the office. Rupe, call her and let her know we're coming. I'll call Shane."

They both whipped out their phones and ten minutes later the car pulled into Taylor's condo building in Brentwood. The press cars veered off in surrender at that point, and Daven grunted in satisfaction. Since Taylor was on the way to the office, she wasn't there, but she gave them the numeric code to get in the apartment. As they entered, Rupe discreetly made eye contact with Vance and Martinez, who took the hint and went back out to the foyer and closed the door.

"So," Rupert said with a tense grin as they settled on the couch, "I really thought you were just coming over to tell me the world's worst dad joke back at the house. *A goat with a banana down his throat?*"

Daven cocked his head quizzically. "Dad joke?"

"It's...never mind. Would you kindly let me know what the hell is going on now? Please?"

"Yes. Lester Boyd called me out of the blue. That description...it was something Colbert said to him a long time ago about his informant. I knew right away who he meant, of course."

"Boyd couldn't have told you this earlier? Like months ago? Jesus."

"Apparently not. I don't know what happened to make him change his mind and call me."

"How do you know this isn't a trick? What motivation did he have to call you?" Rupert asked with great reluctance. He hated even mentioning the possibility, but they had to consider it.

"I don't know if it's a trick, and I don't know why he called."

Rupe shook his head. "If it's true…well, I thought Yannick was one of our best. Damn. Did he say anything else?"

"Yes, and this strictly stays between you and me. I mean it. You cannot tell a single soul. Promise me."

"I promise," Rupert gulped.

Daven stood and took his coat off, then folded it over the arm of the chair and sat back down.

"Turns out the reason Hank agreed to execution was because Harmon agreed to turn the boys over to me after one year if he pled guilty and died for it. Otherwise, he was going to drag out the trial forever. It's clear the boys would have ended up indentured for life if so, considering what we've learned since then."

"What the…so, Harmon basically extorted him."

"Yes. I'm assuming the FBI wasn't aware of that detail, because it's incredibly illegal, needless to say. Either that, or…."

"Or what?"

Daven took his time answering, knowing his very words were treasonous to the core. "Or the FBI was complicit in this scheme all along. Possibly even the president, too."

"What the fuck?" exclaimed Rupert as he leaped to his feet. "Wait, this is too much. I need time to process."

"I know. Regardless whether I'm right or not, if I take Harmon down, he loses control of the deeds. They'll be transferred to the state automatically, not to me."

Rupert went deathly pale. "Shit. You're right. What are you going to do if we can't vindicate Hank, then?" he asked hoarsely.

"I don't know. And without Stewart..." He didn't need to say the rest.

"Jesus, Dav. Do you think Lester Boyd was in on it, too?"

Daven nodded. "That was my first thought the moment I heard he was the negotiator. You know who his boss is now? Colbert. You know who his boss used to be during the revolution? Colbert. Then Hank changed sides and they all threatened to kill each other. It all seems very conveniently lined up to settle some scores, doesn't it?"

Rupe thought about it for a few minutes while they sat together in silence. "Look, that's honestly, that is just an insane theory. Maybe some things line up, yes, but the more you look at it, there more problems there are with it. Stewart and Hank were friends, and...no, I just can't-"

They both jumped as the door from the foyer into the living room opened and Shane and Taylor came in together.

"Something going on, boss?"

Rupert and Daven exchanged knowing looks with each other.

"Yes," Daven replied calmly. "Quite the emergency. Sorry to pull you away on a Friday night."

Taylor dropped her bag next to the side table and headed toward the kitchen. "Alright then. I'd better grab us a few beers before we get started."

Rupert looked at Daven again. "Can I speak to you alone, please? Sorry Shane, we'll be right back."

They both stood up and went into Taylor's bedroom and shut the door.

"Dav, you know I would never say you're wrong unless I'm one hundred percent sure you're wrong. So that's not what I'm saying, But I have a different theory that you need to hear before we progress."

"What?"

"I think...look, I know Colbert. You don't. We worked together in-"

"Yes, yes, I know. What's your theory?" Daven urged his confidante impatiently.

Rupert took a deep breath. "It's possible Harmon was trying to *save* the boys with his offer. He was the one who wanted to trial to end so quickly. You know I hate him, but this...it's not him. Everything you've told me has Colbert written all over it, Dav. I saw firsthand what he was capable of during the revolution. You didn't come into the picture until after he fell. I was *there* working with him every single day until then. I'm telling you, it wouldn't surprise me at all if Harmon and Stewart end up being the good guys in this mess and had no knowledge of Colbert's hand in it."

Dav stared at him. "That would explain why Stewart kept quiet about the documents in the safe. It would have prolonged the trial."

"It could explain a lot of things if we just take the time to sit down and think about it a little longer before jumping to conclusions. It's possibly even Lester was involved at first but changed sides, or maybe he was just as reeled in as Harmon and only recently started to realize things aren't adding up. Maybe that's why he called you. I don't know."

"Alright. That's a second possibility. The third is that Boyd is lying. Stewart told me he was not as deeply involved as I thought."

"So…a fourth scenario is that Stewart was lying," breathed Rupert shakily.

Daven was looking straight at Rupert now. "Maybe they're both lying. Number five."

Rupe took a deep breath. "Fuck, well..well, let's look at possibility six. We also have to consider…you're not going to like this one at all."

"What could possibly be a worse suggestion than what we already have?" Daven said with a shrug. "Let's hear it before I go jump off the balcony and put myself out of my misery."

Rupert suddenly had tears in his eyes now, which astonished his friend.

"Rupe? What…"

"Don't say that again, please."

Daven took a step closer to his friend, looking contrite and embarrassed. "I'm sorry. I didn't mean it, Rupe. Just frustrated. What's the sixth scenario, please?"

Rupert cleared his throat. "Not a scenario. An option. We have to consider waiting until after April 1 to make any move at all."

"That's…" Dav did the math in his head. "More than six months away."

"Yes," Rupert said shakily. "We wait until you have the boys in your custody. Play it safe. And then…if we have anything a hundred percent solid, we pounce and take Colbert down. Or Harmon, or the whole FBI or whatever. Who knows right now. But if we *don't* get the proof…"

"We let it go," Daven finished for him. "And Floyd and Theo remain Bonded Retainers in my house for 19 years."

"Yes."

"No."

Rupert nodded and wiped his eyes. "Just…promise me you'll seriously think about it. We don't have Stewart's support anymore. Salome and Rickon aren't your friends. So if we jump the gun and we're *right* , and Harmon loses those deeds…hell, even if we're wrong he could refuse to turn them over if he thinks you're after him. Let's just say that I very much doubt this alleged agreement exists anywhere in writing. If all we have to do is wait another six months before we make our move, isn't that worth it? The boys are at a boarding school with Lester Boyd, they'll be alright."

Daven turned away and rubbed his temples hard. "I don't know what to do. Do you suggest we stop investigating Yannick until I decide, then?"

"Not at all. If you decide to wait, I say we lay him off with a nice severance package so he can't do any more damage, or get suspicious, and then we take our time backtracking through everything he's ever said and done while he was with us."

"We can't just lay him off and keep everyone else. Talk about creating suspicion."

"We'd have to reorganize the entire department, then."

Dav sighed. "Another cover-up to cover another cover-up. Great."

"Basically, yes. Remember who we're doing this for. Two innocent teenagers who probably don't even know their dad is dead right now."

Daven said nothing for a long time. He just stared at a painting on the bedroom wall. Through it, rather.

Rupe prompted eventually, "Taylor and Shane are waiting for us."

"I know. Hank would know exactly what to do already. He'd be planning every step. I'm not him. I'm...not sure what to do." He sighed heavily.

"He would have already gone in with guns blazing, making some stupid impetuous decision that got us all dug in deeper shit than we started with. So yeah, thank god you're not him."

Daven finally looked at Rupe. "He wasn't *always* like that."

"Yes, he was. You were his voice of reason, and I have always trusted you to do the right thing. You always have. So whatever you decide, I'm all in."

Daven nodded, a bit overcome by emotion for a few seconds, then went back to staring at the painting. All he could think about were the times when he *hadn't* done the right thing. The receipts he'd held onto, for starters.

Rupert cleared his throat roughly. "Time to make a decision, Dav."

Daven shuddered a little. "We're going to wait. Let's tell Shane and Taylor it was a false alarm. Go ahead and send them home."

"You're...this is Taylor's house, so we're the ones who need to go home," Rupert said gently, without any snark. "Are you sure you want to make a decision this quickly? Maybe you should think on it some more."

"No. If the FBI couldn't pin down Colbert's involvement in six months, it's arrogant to think I'll be able to do so on my own."

"But we have Yannick now."

"It's not worth the risk. We'll do the reorganization and get rid of him that way. After I get the boys, we look into his actions. Not before then."

"Dav, I respect your decision and won't say anything more as long as you can assure me you are okay with potentially letting Colbert get away with framing Hank and-"

"Hank's dead, Rupert!" Daven replied hotly. "Forget him now. We can't risk giving Harmon a reason to change his mind about handing those deeds over. If we expose Yannick, we endanger Harmon. Not worth it. Period."

Rupe nodded approvingly. "My thoughts exactly. Just wanted to make sure we were on the same page."

"Oh...that's why you were arguing against your own idea."

"Devil's advocate and all. Someone's got to play the part. I told you I'd be all in, and I am."

"Alright. Let's go home, Rupe."

CHAPTER SEVEN

Los Angeles

"Well you asked me to talk, so now I'm talking."

Harmon closed his eyes in pain and shifted the phone to his other ear. "I've changed my mind. I want you to stop."

"Why?" Daven asked nonchalantly. "You are the one who said I can't ignore you forever."

"On policy matters, yes. You're basically just antagonizing me for the fun of it right now, which I really don't appreciate."

"I have an idea, then."

"What?"

Daven smiled to himself. "Maybe if you take your tiny little hands off your tiny little dick, you can use them to cover your ears so you can't hear me anymore."

"Fuck you, Daven. You're never getting the deeds now."

BEEEEEP. BEEEEEEP. BEEEEEP. BEEEEEEP.

Daven groggily reached over to slam his hand down on his alarm clock for the second time. For several long moments he wasn't sure where he was, until the rapidly increasing movement of Shannon's ticklish tail against his feet caught his attention and eventually brought him back home.

"Hey sweetie," Dav said with a dry grumble as he reached over and scratched her head, then cracked one eye open. She inched up closer to him on her belly - like a soldier crawling under a barbed wire obstacle course, Daven mused idly - and lay alongside him with wide eyes. Time for breakfast, or perhaps she really needed to poop. Both, most likely.

He felt the bed bounce once, and then twice, as the other two dogs jumped up and joined in the plea for their human to rise. Daven closed his eyes again, but he was wide awake already. Today was the day he had agreed to finally speak with Harmon after eight months of avoiding any kind of contact with the Urbanes, and to say he wasn't looking forward to it was a massive understatement. He reached over for his cell phone and dialed Rupert.

"Hey, boss. Did you finally get some sleep, I hope?"

"Yeah."

"Today's the day," Rupe reminded him unnecessarily.

"I know. I was just dreaming about how badly the conversation might go. Rupe..."

"Don't chicken out, Dav. You got this. You've been rehearsing for weeks."

Daven looked at his three dogs. No...his dog, and Floyd and Theo's two dogs. The latter two's happiness depended on every move he made next.

"Listen, I have to tell you something important. Are you alone?"

"Yes."

Daven took a deep breath. "I got a hold of Stewart last night. Finally."

There was a long pause on the other end. "You agreed not to drag him back into-"

"I know. Just listen. He confirmed the deal was legit, that the boys are mine again on April 1. I just...I wanted to thank you, Rupe. For convincing me to wait. You were right. But now I have a favor to ask you, and you're not going to like it."

Rupert took a deep breath, then picked his coffee back up. "Is this request going to result in an argument, by chance?"

"Yes."

"Fuck. Not sure I've had enough coffee yet."

Daven ignored that. "If Rickon doesn't confirm me tomorrow as new leader of the party, I want you to start the proceedings to take over."

"No."

"Rupe-"

"I said no, Dav, and that's the end of it." Rupert went to the other end of his office and shut the door hard. "You go, I go. End of story. Besides, he has no reason not to confirm you."

"Even if he does, I'm not sure I even want to bring the boys back into this life. You know what it's like, Rupe. I work 14 hours a day. It's not fair to them. Hank was…he was so absent from their lives, and never knew most of the time where they were or what they were up to. I can't do that to them. I should quit."

"Under different circumstances, yes. But you've forgotten one thing."

"What?"

Rupert took another deep breath. "Don't hate me for saying it, Dav. But it's got to be said. They're not your sons."

"I'm aware of that."

"They'll be your servants."

"Yes," Daven huffed. "As if I could possibly need another reminder. What's your point?"

"You know what my point is. They have to live by certain guidelines, or you're going to be in serious shit. You can't take them out sailing, or to museums, or what have you. Exactly what kind of quality time do you plan on having?"

"I'm not going to get into that right now," Daven replied calmly. "It's putting the cart before the bridge."

"Horse, Dav. What else did Stewart say?"

"The horse before the bridge, then. You know what I mean."

"It's *cart* before the *horse* . Are you going to tell me what else he said, or are we going to debate metaphors all day?"

"It's an idiom, not a metaphor. He also said he was fined an enormous amount by the FBI for his role in the ending the Colbert investigation prematurely."

"As we figured. Damn. Did you tell him about Yannick?"

"No, that was all. He hung up on me after saying he was going to block my number. That was literally our entire conversation, unfortunately. But what he did tell me was huge, and makes me feel a lot better about dealing with Harmon now."

Daven paused as he heard the incoming call beep on his phone. Speak of the devil.

"What the hell?" he wondered aloud. "He's calling me now."

"Did you have the time wrong? Forget to account for time zones, or whatever?"

"No. Hold on."

Daven clicked over to the other line.

"Johansson."

"Daven, sorry to call earlier than scheduled. I was hoping we can meet in person instead of over the phone."

"Um. When?"

"Today. I'm in San Diego and can send my jet up for you."

And crash it into the side of a mountain just for kicks. "No, thank you. Phone is fine."

"It's incredibly important, and for your ears only," Harmon urged. "But I can't come up to Los Angeles, for the same reasons you won't go to Denver."

"I'm not going to San Diego, either."

There was a sigh on the other line. "Fine. Palm Springs?"

"No. I will consider Temecula. There's a vineyard there with private space. The manager is a good friend of mine and very discreet. That's your only option. Take it or leave it."

"I'll take it. 2pm?"

"That's fine. I'll email you with details."

"No. Call me back. Put nothing in writing to me or to your friend. What's the name of the vineyard?"

"Ponte Inn. May I ask, why do you-"

The line went dead, and Daven held the phone and stared at it like it was made of lava. "What the..." Then he remembered Rupert was still on the other line, and he clicked back over.

"Sorry, Rupert. He just wanted to reconfirm the time of our meeting." Daven flushed a little; he hated lying to his friend but he wasn't quite sure yet what had just happened, and wasn't willing to admit he'd made a rash decision to meet his rival in person. Secretly, no less.

"Did you manage to do that without pissing him off?"

"Of course. I'd better go. Lots to prepare, and I haven't read over the policy documents enough to memorize the big points. I'll do the call from home."

"I think that's for the best," agreed Rupert. "No chance of anyone overhearing anything. But please do call me right after and tell me everything."

"I will, of course."

Seditionists HQ - Los Angeles

1pm

Rupert sighed for what seemed like the hundredth time today as he pored over more newspaper articles relating to the rumors that Hank was no longer among the living. The FBI had of course said nothing, and neither had the Seditionists. Daven had a brief call with Salome to discuss, but she was certain that it was all idle speculation and not an information leak. Rupert wasn't so sure, but so far, nobody seemed to be taking it very seriously. That made him feel a little better, but not much.

His concentration was suddenly broken by a knock on his door, and he hit the button on his desk that unlocked it remotely. "Yes? Come in."

His assistant came in and handed him a packet. "Courier just came by and dropped this off for you and Daven."

"Thank you." Rupert waited until she was gone and then ripped the packet open, and then picked up the phone to call Dav, who didn't answer.

"Dav, we just got something at the office you need to see for your call with…for your 2pm call, rather. The updated measures for December, and it's way too big to fax over. Looks like quite a few changes in verbiage you two will need to discuss. Call me back."

Rupert rang for Taylor, who came immediately. "Sorry to turn you into an errand girl, but I need you to take this over to Daven's house immediately. He'll need it for a 2pm conference call he's taking from home. Use my driver. Thanks, love."

Rupert went back to his coffee and articles, and thought nothing else of it until Taylor called him 45 minutes later.

"Hey Taylor, everything okay?"

"No," Taylor replied, a little bewildered. "He's not home."

Rupert looked at his watch; it was nearly time for the call. "What? Are you sure?"

"I'm certain. He has one guard on watch, but the car and other two guards are gone. Toby said he was too busy for visitors, but he's obviously not there. I'm waiting outside just in case he shows up. If he doesn't, what do you want me to do with this?"

"I'll call you right back."

Rupe called Dav at the house and on his cell, but only got the option to leave a voicemail. Then he tried Martinez, and Vance. Both went straight to voicemail. Now he was alarmed, and made the decision to call Shane in telecommunications for assistance.

"Yes, boss?"

"Sorry to bother you, Shane. I can't get a hold of Daven and it's critical. Can you let me know if his phone is turned on?"

"Sure. One moment."

Rupert swallowed hard; it wasn't odd for Dav to ignore everyone and disappear off the radar when he got overly focused on a task. But him not being home for such a crucial phone call, not to mention both his guards unreachable as well? That was another story...

"Sir?" Shane sounded concerned.

"Yeswhatisit?" Rupert blurted quickly.

"I'm showing his phone is not turned off, physically, but it doesn't have a signal. He's out of range."

"What? *Out of range?* Where was it last located?"

"I can't...you know it's against policy for me to tell you that, sir."

Rupert smiled a little; he was the one who had written the policy. "It's a matter of his personal safety, Shane. I take complete responsibility and will report it to Daven myself. Where was the phone last detected?"

There was a telling pause. "Can you send an authorization email first, please?"

"Of course." Rupert reached over to his laptop and yanked up the lid, then banged out a quick message to both men explaining what he had just asked Shane to do, taking great care to emphasize that Shane had first refused exactly as protocol demanded.

"Sent. Tell me when you receive it."

"Received, thank you. I'm showing that phone last pinged a cell tower in Temecula 17 minutes ago. Let me check the address....that tower is located at the intersection of Meadows Parkway and Rancho California Road. That doesn't mean it's exactly where he was, he could be anywhere within a few miles of it."

Rupert knew exactly where he was, cell phone tower be damned. He was meeting with Harmon in person at Ponte Inn...in secret, for some reason. As if that wasn't bad enough, he would learn afterwards that Rupert was spying on him and it wasn't really a secret at all.

Fuck. I'll be lucky to have a job at all after today, never mind what Rickon says...

"Alright, thanks Shane. That explains what I needed to know. Appreciate it," Rupert finally said in a strangled tone. "Have a nice afternoon."

Temecula, 2pm

Daven set down his briefcase as he entered the small boardroom, where he found Harmon awaiting him. The man looked incredibly nervous for a change, and Dav wasn't sure what to make of it. His own heart started beating overly fast in response.

"Good day," he said politely as he took off his coat and sat down. He wanted to ask what the hell was so important about the December measures that required a last-second, in-person meeting, but he refrained with some difficulty.

"Good afternoon," responded Harmon. "Is this room bugged, or do you have any recording devices on you?"

"No to both questions. Are *you* recording us?"

"No."

Daven didn't touch the papers he had brought along. "I take it we're not going to be discussing the December measures."

"I don't know if we'll have time."

"You're nervous," Daven observed calmly. "Why?"

Harmon shifted in his chair, then picked up a pen and started tapping it on the table. "I know you hate me, Daven. For what happened to Hank, and all that. Can't say I blame you."

"*All that?*" Dav echoed mockingly. "Bit of an understatement, don't you think?"

"Perhaps, yes. I think that the way everything went down was tragic, but for the best. Just my opinion, with which you obviously disagree."

Daven didn't take his eyes off his enemy. "I'm curious. What gave you the idea that your *opinion* matters to me?"

Harmon laughed nervously, then set his pen down. "Alright. I can see Hank rubbed off on you more than I thought. I'm not going to fight with you. I...what I'm about to tell you is going to cost both of us our jobs, most likely. If you don't want to hear it, you should leave now."

Now it was Daven's turn to squirm in his chair. "I'm listening."

"Alright. I was in a meeting with Colbert yesterday, and he left his cell phone behind. I was taking it to him when it rang."

"Okay."

"And because I was a little distracted, I picked it up, thinking it was my own."

"Who was it?"

Harmon swallowed hard. "One of my former operatives whom Colbert had assured me we were no longer in contact with. I mean, for like...ten months. Asking for payment from me for his latest services to the Urbanes that I supposedly authorized."

Daven stared the man down hard. "You told the FBI and Hank that you had no more double agents. In fact, you used that claim to force us to disband our own counter-intelligence operations."

"Now we get down to why I'm so nervous. This proves, as I suspected months ago, that Colbert is running his own operation without my knowledge. It goes without saying that Stewart leaving the FBI was the fatal blow in my attempt to prove it."

"I see. A minute ago you said that this information would cost both of us our jobs. You, yes, but I don't see what I have to do with it."

"Right. Well, that's where the next part comes in. I know you've been in contact with Lester Boyd, contrary to the terms of the confidentiality agreement you signed with the FBI. Simply put, I won't hesitate to blow the whistle on you if you don't answer my next question truthfully."

Daven sat up straighter in his chair, his chest tight with anxiety and impending sense of doom. He couldn't even say anything back, he was *that* flabbergasted.

Harmon continued calmly, "I want to know exactly why this man was laid off. My suspicion is that you somehow became aware of his activities, or at least suspected him of being a mole."

"I want to know how *you know* he was laid off, since you claim to not be in contact with him anymore."

"Colbert told me some time ago when I asked if we could possibly use the man's services again. I asked only to see what he'd say, and had no intention of actually carrying it through."

Daven desperately wanted to flee the room. It was getting hot.

"I don't know what you want," he said finally.

"To bring down Colbert. You have at least some kind of proof of the scheme, and you know what that could mean. I'll give you a few minutes to think about it anyway," Harmon said dangerously, in control again. He was always a hundred times more intimidating when the ball was in his court.

"Answer me first," Daven responded, his tone edgy and hard. "What *services* did he want payment for, exactly?"

"I don't know, and that's the truth. From what little he said, it's clear he genuinely thinks I'm in on the whole thing. I'm not, needless to say, but I played along long enough to allay his suspicion. So why did you separate him from your company? Did you get an inkling of what he was doing?”

Daven raised an eyebrow. “Let’s get one thing clear first, Harmon. I’m not impressed by your threats. I have no interest in what blackmail designs you have in mind. What I want to do is bring down Colbert, and if I can help you do that, I’m all in. But you need to give me something, first. Otherwise I can’t trust you with a single word out of my mouth.”

Harmon looked at him out of the sides of his eyes. “What could you possibly want more than my silence?”

“The deeds to Theo and Floyd. *Now*, not on April 1. I’ll pay the penalty for early transfer, whatever it is, I don’t care. Just see it done and I’ll give you all the information you want.”

“No. They’ll be the only leverage I have left if this goes south.”

“Leverage? They’re *kids!*”

Harmon scoffed. “Oh come on, you’re just as guilty as I am trying to use them as a bargaining chip. Didn’t you literally just ask me to trade them over in exchange for information?”

Daven rolled his eyes, knowing he was defeated on that point. Then he ripped a piece of paper from his notebook and tore it in half, giving one to Harmon.

“You’re right. But let’s get started off correctly. We don’t even know if we’re talking about the same person. Write down this alleged mole’s name. I’ll do the same. Then we exchange papers and open them at the same time. If the names are different, I leave now and we'll never speak of this again. If they're the same, I'll cooperate with you. Agreed?"

Harmon nodded. "You do realize that if the names are different, you'll end up with the knowledge of two possible moles, and I'll have absolutely nothing?"

"Nothing? You mean, like what I'm getting out of this if the names are the same? Write it down."

Harmon obliged grudgingly, then passed his folded up paper over to Daven at the same time he received one.

Daven looked down at what was handed to him, and his heart flipped as he read it:

Yannick

He looked across the table to Harmon, who un-folded his own paper and looked down at it. He seemed stunned as he set it face down on the table, very slowly.

"Alright. It seems I owe you an apology," he said quietly. "Bringing you out here for nothing. But at least you know you had two moles now, and who they are. I have no fucking clue how to proceed now."

Daven stood up and started to put his coat on. "Well, I suppose I should thank you for trying. At least we agree on one thing. Colbert is a dangerous, manipulative liar."

"He's not the only one. Takes one to know one, am I right?"

Dav paused, one arm in and one arm out of his coat. "What's that supposed to mean?"

"Oh, nothing. It's just...the name I gave you? It's real. The one you gave me is fake, isn't it? Andrew P., really? Generic much?"

Oh, shit. "What makes you think it's fake?" Daven scoffed offhandedly, although his cheeks started to flush as Harmon sat back with a smug expression and crossed his arms.

"Is it for real?"

"Yes, that's him. Obviously I didn't give the last name for privacy's sake."

"Hmm. Funny thing. I didn't think it was fake at first, actually. Just thought I'd throw it out there to see what happens. Did you know you blush like a little girl when you lie?"

Daven did know that, actually. It had caused much embarrassment in the past. "I'm not lying."

"Another lie, and you're getting even darker. Look, Daven, I get it. You don't trust me, and I don't blame you. But there's one thing I want you to know before you go."

"What?"

Harmon uncrossed his arms and laid his hands flat on the table. "I may be an insufferable, annoying, smug piece of shit to you. But I saved those boys from a *lifetime* of servitude, and that's the truth. You know who condemned them first, though? It wasn't Colbert, and it certainly wasn't me."

He meant Hank, of course. Daven nodded. "I know that Hank...did some things," he admitted.

"Yes, he did. But what compelled him to do those things in the first place?"

Daven looked at the floor and thought about it. "Colbert, I suppose, when it all boils down to it. Goes way back."

"Correct. Chicken and the egg, Daven. They were each other's own worst enemies."

"Don't lecture me."

"The cycle was broken when Hank paid the price, but I'm not going to let Colbert get away with it. Especially since what he's done is going to be the end of me, too. I know that prospect cheers you. So I'm going to ask again...why did you suspect Yannick was working with him?"

Daven continued staring at the floor for a minute, then slowly removed his coat and sat back down into the chair. After a moment, he pulled the desk phone over and positioned it exactly in between both of them.

"If we're doing this, we're doing it properly and calling Salome together. Right now. The first thing you're going to tell her is that you're signing the deeds over to Rupert today."

"Rupert? Not you?"

"Correct. I'll have to tell her about my involvement with Lester Boyd in order to explain how I got the intel on Yannick. But I'd rather go to jail than keep those boys in servitude for one more day in an Urbanes indoctrination center. Understood?"

Harmon looked aghast. "That's not what it is. Wait a minute…just a second. *Lester Boyd* told you it was Yannick?"

"Not directly. I'll explain it to her. Are we proceeding, or not?"

Harmon inhaled sharply, realizing that Daven had no idea Lester held the deeds to the boys. If they got Boyd in trouble…well, shit. Then he may not release the deeds out of spite, or even lose them outright. But if Daven knew that, he would never in a million years cooperate at this point. All he had to do was wait until April 1, after all, and the boys were his. Harmon held out his hand and decided not to mention that little detail.

"Yes. I've got your back, and I expect you to have mine. If you can agree to that, then let's do it."

Daven shook it after significant hesitation. Then Harmon started dialing Salome while Dav did everything in his power not to vomit all over the table.

THREE HOURS LATER

Daven looked at his phone's emails for the first time when they were almost near the house, and he practically exploded when he saw that Rupert had been tracking his location.

"You've got to be kidding me," he muttered angrily, and Martinez looked back at him over the headrest.

"Sorry, sir?"

Daven put down his phone. "Nothing. Did you have any missed calls from Rupert today?"

"Yes, sir. There was no signal at the meeting complex."

"Okay. Let's swing by his house, please. I'll only need a minute, so wait in the car."

"Shall we alert his guards that you're coming?"

"Yes, please." Daven had the habit of springing up on people unexpectedly, although he didn't intend to. He just assumed the other person would know, naturally.

Rupert was waiting at the front door when they pulled up, and he silently led Daven to his study. Both men were bursting at the seams with anger and confusion.

"Don't ever track me again," Daven began, then held up a hand when Rupert started to protest. "That's the end of it. No need to explain, no need to apologize. Just don't repeat the mistake."

"Fine. Do you care to explain why you ran off and secretly met with Harmon in a non-secure location? This is bullshit, Dav, you can't do that to me. I'm supposed to know everything."

"Calm down. You're officially on the know-nothing list as of right now. My meeting with Harmon wasn't about the measures, that's all I'm going to say."

"What the-"

"Quiet, please. There's something I have to tell you. It couldn't wait until morning."

Rupert did calm down, although, he hated to be told to calm down. That only made things worse, but something in Daven's bearing stopped him from blowing up any further.

"What's wrong?" he asked in genuine concern, and not a little fear.

"I'm sorry to do this to you, Rupert, I really am."

"Are you...are you *firing* me, Dav?"

Daven looked askance at him. "What? No. God, I wish it was just that."

"*Just that?* Okay, what the hell is going on?"

"Is your basement still equipped for servant's quarters?"

"Uh…we haven't gotten around to remodeling the rooms, but they're being used as storage for the moment. Why would you ask such a thing?"

Daven reached into his jacket and started to hand over a poor copy of a fax that had already been almost unreadable to start with.

"What is this? I can't make it out."

"Deeds. I'll have to explain later, but the boys belong to you now. Floyd and Theo, I mean. Can you put the rooms back in order for them? They should arrive within 48 hours, but I don't have their flight information yet. When I do, I'll pass it along."

Rupert didn't take the paper. He was white as a ghost.

"Dav…what in the holy fuck is going on. Tell me right now."

Daven looked him in the eyes and said matter-of-factly, "I can't. Please just take good care of them until I get things all sorted out. I'm flying to Richmond tonight to collect them in the morning and see them off, then I'll be in Philadelphia for the rest of the week."

"Are you…holy shit, did you get arrested?"

"Not yet, but the possibility is there until I can get some things cleared up. That's why I didn't have the deeds transferred to me."

Rupert was astonished to see Daven actually smiling a little. He was...was he *happy*? Happy about *what*?

"Have you been drinking, Dav?"

"No." His smile fell off abruptly. "Rupert, I need help with something else. I'm going to have to tell them about Hank before they find out on their own. If you have any ideas...I have no idea what to say."

Rupert shook his head. "Regardless, you can't just drop a bomb like that and then put them on a plane by themselves. I'm coming with you and we'll talk about it on the way over, and I'll fly back with them. What time are you leaving?"

"In two hours. We'll pick you up, of course. Are you sure?"

"Yes. Let me get packed and tell Millie what's happening. Call me when you're about ten minutes away."

"I will. Thanks, Rupe," Daven said warmly, and they gave each other a small but manly hug.

"Sorry for my initial response, but it was quite the shock. Of course we're thrilled to have Theo and Floyd back. It's going to be strange, though...wow. Servants. I can't wrap my brain around it."

"Me either. See you in two hours."

"Dav?" Rupe called as his friend started to walk away.

"Yes?"

"We're taking a private plane, I'm guessing?"

Daven nodded.

"You should bring the dogs," Rupe said firmly. "They're the best kind of therapy."

"Good idea. Thanks. See you soon."